D1470077

King Gorboduc's Fabulous Zoo

STEPHEN BOSWELL

King Gorboduc's Fabulous Zoo

illustrated by
BEVERLEY GOODING

E. P. DUTTON • NEW YORK

for Zöe, Lucy and Rupert

Text copyright © 1986 by Stephen Boswell
Illustrations copyright © 1986 by Beverley Gooding

All rights reserved. No part of this publication may be
reproduced or transmitted in any form or by any means,
electronic or mechanical, including photocopy, recording,
or any information storage and retrieval system now
known or to be invented, without permission in writing
from the publisher, except by a reviewer who wishes to
quote brief passages in connection with a review written
for inclusion in a magazine, newspaper, or broadcast.

Published in the United States by E. P. Dutton,
2 Park Avenue, New York, N.Y. 10016

Originally published in Great Britain in 1986
by Methuen Children's Books Ltd
11 New Fetter Lane, London EC4P 4EE

Printed in Singapore   OBE   First Edition
ISBN: 0-525-44267-7   10 9 8 7 6 5 4 3 2 1

King Gorboduc had a private zoo of which he was very proud. In the zoo there was a Unicorn, a Griffin, a Dodo and a baby Mammoth.

The Unicorn looked like this –
It was the only Unicorn in the World.

The Griffin looked like this –
It was the only Griffin in the World.

The Dodo looked like this –
It was the only Dodo in the World.

The baby Mammoth looked like this –
It was the only baby Mammoth in the World.

Although King Gorboduc was proud of his zoo he was not satisfied.
'What my zoo needs is a dragon,' he declared.

The Chief Courtier stepped forward and proudly told the King that he knew of a dragon who lived in the village of Tottering-on-the-Edge.

Immediately King Gorboduc ordered his soldiers to march to the village
of Tottering and bring back the dragon.

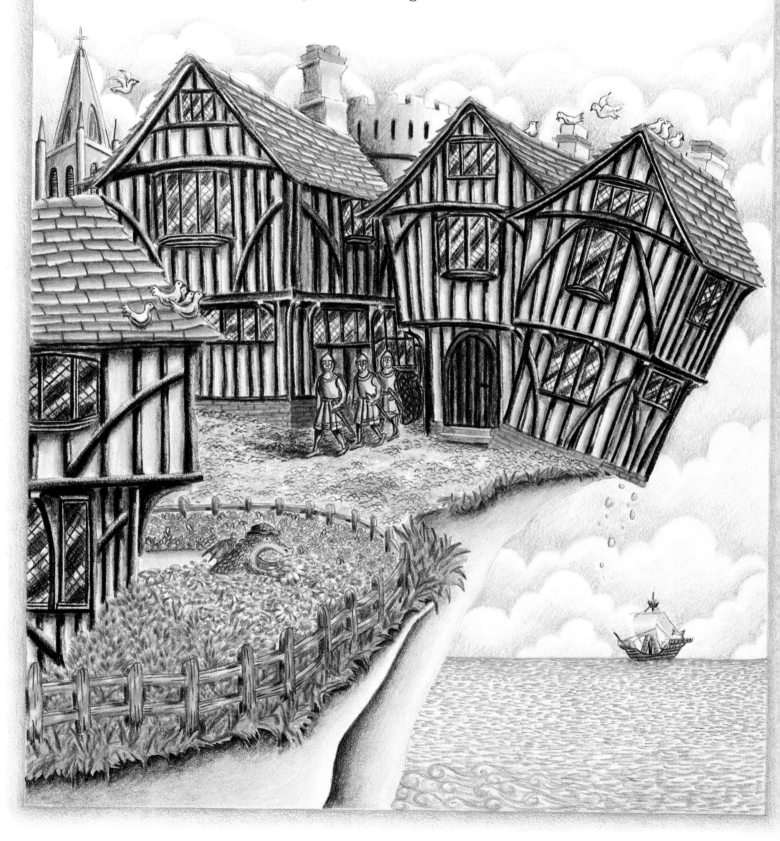

The dragon was a very gentle creature. He lived a quiet life pottering about his garden. He was only happy when he was among his flowers.

The dragon was very upset when he saw the King's soldiers trampling down his chrysanthemums.

But he was even more upset when they threw a net over him and carried him to the King's zoo.

When the soldiers arrived at the zoo they gave the unhappy dragon to Fred, the King's zoo-keeper. Fred felt sorry for the animals in the zoo and tried to do all he could for them.

He would polish the Unicorn's horn –

Brush the Griffin's mane –

Dust the Dodo's mirror —

And read a bed-time story to the baby Mammoth.

The King was delighted with the dragon but he was still not satisfied. He ordered Fred to find him another fabulous beast.

That evening, while he was giving the dragon his supper, Fred had an idea. It was a brilliant plan to free all the animals.

'I shall find the King a Basilisk,' said Fred.

'What's a Basilisk?' asked the Court-Jester.

'It's the King of Serpents,' explained Fred. 'If you look into its face you immediately drop down dead. It looks like this . . .' Fred pulled a hideous face but the Jester was unimpressed.

'All right,' said Fred, 'I shall tell you the whole plan. But first we'd better call all the animals together.'

Fred whispered his plan to the Jester. Then he whispered it to the Unicorn, the Griffin, the Dodo, the Dragon and the baby Mammoth.

Later that night there was much sewing of cloth and mixing of paints in Fred's workshop.

The next morning Fred told the King that he had caught a Basilisk – the most rare of all fabulous beasts. King Gorboduc was overjoyed. He told Fred that he would visit the zoo immediately.

King Gorboduc and his courtiers hurried to the zoo.

'Well, where is it?' the King asked impatiently.

'In this box, Your Majesty,' said Fred.

'Let's see it then!' said the King, trying hard not to look too excited.

'Very well,' said Fred and he opened the lid of a large box.

At once there was a tremendous roar and out of the box rose an enormous and hideous head.

All the animals screamed and fell to the ground. Fred clutched his throat, his face turned purple and he yelled to the King and the courtiers: 'Run for your lives! Don't look at the Basilisk or you will die!' Then he rolled his eyes, gurgled horribly and fell down as if he were dead.

The King and the courtiers did not wait to hear any more but ran as fast as they could through the zoo gates.

They did not stop until they reached the castle. When everyone was inside, the guards raised the drawbridge, lowered the portcullis and then bolted all the doors just in case.

As soon as the last of the courtiers had run from the zoo, Fred and all the animals sat up and cheered. The Basilisk laughed so much that its head fell off revealing the Court-Jester. It had been him all along!

No one came out of the castle for a week. When the bravest courtier did venture out he found that the zoo was empty. There was no sign of the fabulous beasts; there was no sign of Fred and the Jester and, of course, there was no sign of the Basilisk.

Today in the town of Basking-by-the-Sea you will find a 'Home For Retired Fabulous Beasts'. If you look over the garden wall you will see that the gardener is a happy little dragon.